Once Upon A... DRAGON'S FIRE

EX : LIBRIS

THIS BOOK BELONGS TO:

BEATRICE BLUE

Once Upon A
DRAGON'S
FIRE

Frances Lincoln
First Editions

Once upon a magic kingdom, before fire ever existed,
there lived a terrifying dragon near a village.
No one had ever seen the dragon, but
everyone knew all about him.

For it was written in books that...

he was so **mean** he ate kittens for breakfast!

He was so **scary** he made children scream!

And he was so evil that he blew huge storms out of his jaws, which was why it was always so cold.

Everyone was scared of the dragon...

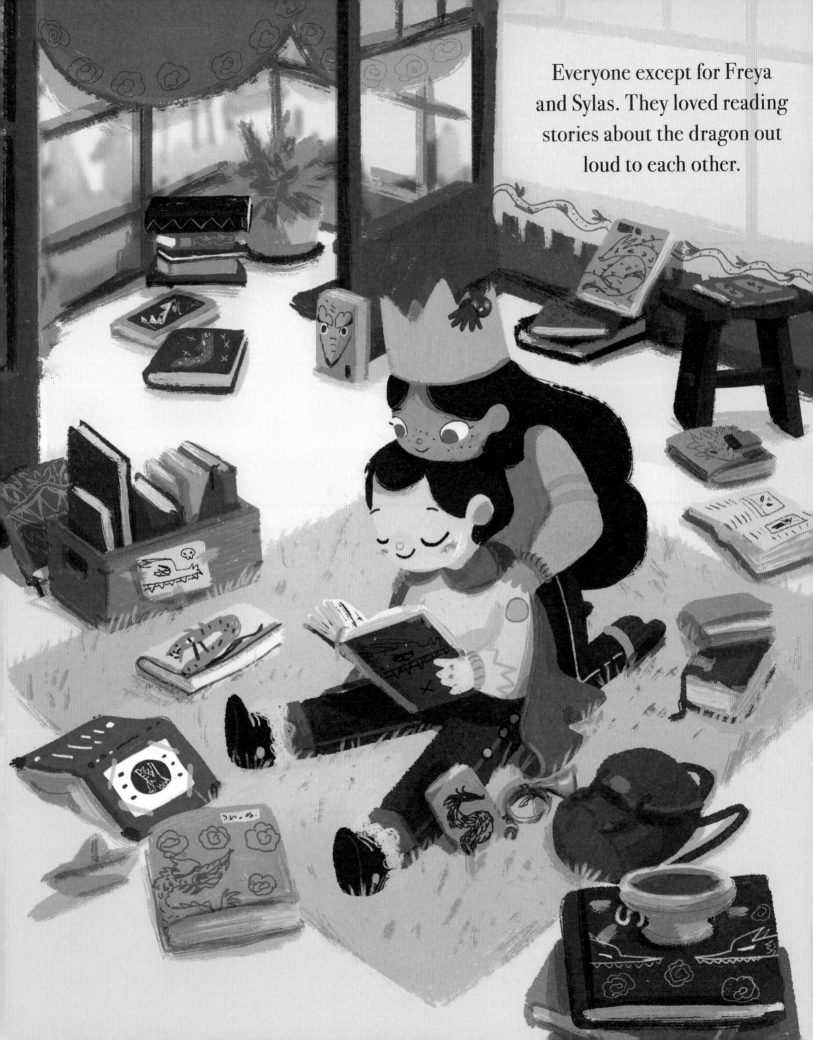

Everyone except for Freya
and Sylas. They loved reading
stories about the dragon out
loud to each other.

"I'm not scared," Sylas would say when
Freya spoke of the dragon's roar, which
was so loud it destroyed roofs.

"I'm not scared either,"
Freya would say, when Sylas read
about the dragon's long, sharp
claws and terrifying teeth.

Reading about the dragon was their favourite thing to do.

One bitter winter day,
a big, big storm began to blow.
It was so cold that all the warmth left the town,
and no one could bring it back.

"This storm must be the dragon's fault!" Sylas said.

"Enough is enough," Freya answered.

"We have to do something."

Both of them were agreed.
"This bad dragon must be stopped!"

So the two of them set off
up the high, windy mountain.

When they got to the
top, they found a cave. Two big
yellow eyes shone out from the dark.
"I'm not scared," Sylas whispered.
They stepped inside...

... and they saw the dragon.

But he didn't have long, sharp claws. He didn't have terrifying teeth. And he didn't roar so loudly that roofs were destroyed.

In fact, this dragon
wasn't scary at all.

He was just cold, scared
and very, very lonely.

"We need to help him!" said Freya.

Freya and Sylas knew that when they felt sad or lonely,
there was one thing that always made them feel better.
So they snuggled close to the dragon and began to read.

But then Sylas realised something terrible.

Every story they knew
said the dragon was evil!
"But that's not true,"
said Sylas.

Then Freya had an idea.
"What if we make up a new
story?" she said.

"Once upon a magic kingdom, there
lived a very **beautiful** dragon,"
Freya said. "Everyone **loved** him
because he was kind.

He always reminded people
to stay together and be good
to one another."

As Dragon listened to the new story,
a warmth started to grow deep in his chest.
The more Freya and Sylas talked, the warmer
and warmer he got, until...

With his new power, Dragon flew down the mountain to
protect everyone in the town from the mighty storm.

He warmed up all their homes . . .

. . . and their
hearts.

From that day on, dragons carry fire
inside, to remind us of something
very important.

That we can only
truly discover something
with our own eyes,

and even on the coldest days, a spark can
come from something as tiny as a new story.

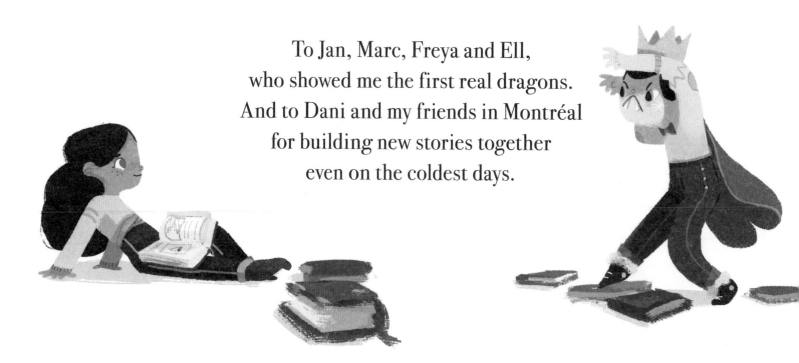

To Jan, Marc, Freya and Ell,
who showed me the first real dragons.
And to Dani and my friends in Montréal
for building new stories together
even on the coldest days.

Brimming with creative inspiration, how-to projects, and useful information to enrich your everyday life, Quarto Knows is a favourite destination for those pursuing their interests and passions. Visit our site and dig deeper with our books into your area of interest: Quarto Creates, Quarto Cooks, Quarto Homes, Quarto Lives, Quarto Drives, Quarto Explores, Quarto Gifts, or Quarto Kids.

Text and illustrations © 2020 Beatrice Blue

First published in 2020 by Frances Lincoln Children's Books.
First published in paperback in 2020 by Frances Lincoln Children's Books, an imprint of the Quarto Group.
The Old Brewery, 6 Blundell Street, London N7 9BH, United Kingdom.
T (0)20 7700 6700 F (0)20 7700 8066
www.QuartoKnows.com

ISBN 978-1-78603-554-7
eISBN 978-1-78603-555-4

The illustrations were created digitally
Set in Bodoni 72

Published and edited by Katie Cotton
Designed by Zoë Tucker
Production by Caragh McAleenan
Manufactured in Guangdong, China EB062020
1 3 5 7 9 8 6 4 2

MIX
Paper from
responsible sources
FSC® C124385

EX LIBRIS

There are more magical adventures to be had in
Beatrice Blue's first book:

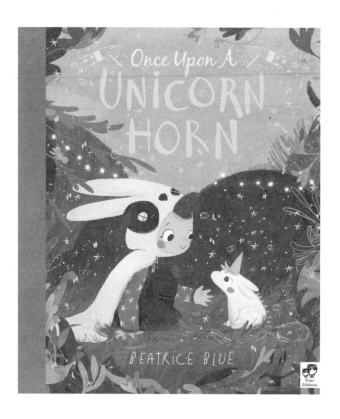

Once Upon a Unicorn Horn

ISBN: 978-1-78603-589-9

Do you know how unicorns got their horns? It
all began once upon a magic forest, when a little
girl called June discovered tiny horses learning
how to fly in her garden. But one of the poor
horses couldn't fly at all! So, with the help of her
parents, June thought of a very sweet and very
delicious way to make her new friend happy...